D0852914

Dear Parent:
Your child's love of reading starts here!

Every child learns to read in a different way and at his or her own speed. You can help your young reader improve and become more confident by encouraging his or her own interests and abilities. You can also guide your child's spiritual development by reading stories with biblical values and Bible stories, like I Can Read! books published by Zonderkidz. From books your child reads with you to the first books he or she reads alone, there are I Can Read! books for every stage of reading:

SHARED READING
Basic language, word repetition, and whimsical illustrations, ideal for sharing with your emergent reader.

BEGINNING READING
Short sentences, familiar words, and simple concepts for children eager to read on their own.

READING WITH HELP
Engaging stories, longer sentences, and language play for developing readers.

READING ALONE
Complex plots, challenging vocabulary, and high-interest topics for the independent reader.

ADVANCED READING
Short paragraphs, chapters, and exciting themes for the perfect bridge to chapter books.

I Can Read! books have introduced children to the joy of reading since 1957. Featuring award-winning authors and illustrators and a fabulous cast of beloved characters, I Can Read! books set the standard for beginning readers.

A lifetime of discovery begins with the magical words **"I Can Read!"**

Visit www.icanread.com for information on enriching your child's reading experience. Visit www.zonderkidz.com for more Zonderkidz I Can Read! titles.

I have set my rainbow in the clouds, and it
will be the sign of the covenant between me
and the earth.
—*Genesis 9:13*

ZONDERKIDZ

Heroes of the Bible Treasury
Copyright © 2016 by Zondervan
Illustrations © 2016 by David Miles

Requests for information should be addressed to:

Zonderkidz, 3900 Sparks Drive SE, Grand Rapids, Michigan 49546

ISBN 978-0-310-75096-3 (hardcover)

Noah's Voyage (2015) 978-0-310-74683-6
Joseph the Dreamer (2015) 978-0-310-75084-0
Moses Leads the People (2014) 978-0-310-73236-5
Elijah, God's Mighty Prophet (2016) 978-0-310-75081-9
Brave Queen Esther (2015) 978-0-310-74666-9
Paul Meets Jesus (2016) 978-0-310-75076-5

Editor: Mary Hassinger
Art direction and design: Kris Nelson

Printed in China

16 17 18 19 20 21 /DHC / 21 20 19 18 17 16 15 14 13 12 11 10 9 8 7 6 5 4 3 2 1

Adventure BIBLE

Noah's Voyage

Pictures by David Miles

It was quiet in Noah's tent.

Everyone was sleeping.

Noah was thinking about his voyage

on the ark.

One day, God came to Noah.

God said, "Noah, you are my friend.

I love you. Please help me."

Noah answered, "Yes, Lord.

I will do whatever you say."

God said, "The people on earth
do not follow my rules.
I am sorry I made man.
But you are a good man, Noah."
"How can I help?" asked Noah.

God said, "There is going to be a flood.
Build an ark. Then two of every creature,
one male and one female, will come.
Put them on the ark. Then wait."

Noah did everything God asked.
Noah's sons Shem, Ham, and Jephath
helped build the ark too.

Noah and his family worked very hard.

God knew he made the right choice.

Noah and his family did the job just right.

God said, "Good work, my friend.

Now all the animals will come.

Put them on the ark. Then you get on too.

The flood will come very soon,"

God said.

So the animals came to Noah.

God sent every kind of living creature.

There were birds, monkeys,
alligators, dogs, bumblebees,
and more ...

Some animals went on the top floor.

Some animals went on the middle floor.

Some animals went on the bottom floor.

Then Noah and his family—his wife,

his sons, and their wives—got on the ark.

God closed the window tight.

Noah was 600 years old when

the floodwaters came!

Rain fell on the earth

for forty days and forty nights.

The waters covered everything on earth.

But the water did not cover Noah

and his family.

God kept them safe.

The animals on the ark were safe too.

Noah and his family took care

of the animals.

And they took care of each other.

Even when the rain stopped,
the earth was flooded for 150 days.
God said, "Don't worry, Noah.
You, your family, and the animals
will stay safe."

Noah knew God loved them very much.

He knew they would be safe.

After 150 days, the water started
going down!
After even more days, the ark
came to rest on the tops of
the mountains of Ararat.

Noah opened a window.

He sent a raven to fly

through the air.

"Go! Look for dry land!" said Noah.

Next, Noah sent out a dove to
look for dry land.

But the dove came back.

Noah said, "It is fine, little dove.
We will try again soon."

Seven days later the dove went out

the window again.

When it came back, it had

a fresh olive leaf in its beak.

"You did it, little dove!"

Noah shouted.

When Noah was 601 years old,

the water dried up.

God said, "Come out of the ark, Noah!

Bring your family and the animals!"

All the animals and Noah went out onto the dry land to live and grow again.

On dry land, Noah built an altar
to honor God.

Noah and his family said thank
you to God for keeping them safe.

Then God did something
wonderful.

He put a rainbow in the sky.

God promised to never flood
the earth ever again.

And Noah knew God
would keep his promise.

I will establish my covenant with you.
—*Genesis 6:18*

Noah

Noah was a good man. When all other men were making God unhappy, he loved and believed in God. So when God needed help, he went to Noah and asked him to build the ark. Noah said yes. Noah trusted God and knew that it was the right thing to do.

Did You Know?

God gave Noah very detailed instructions on how to build the ark. He told Noah to make the ark 300 cubits long, 50 cubits wide, and 30 cubits high. This would be about 1 ½ football fields long and as tall as a five-story building. It needed to have a roof, windows, and a door large enough for the big animals that would go on the voyage. Noah was to use cypress wood and pitch to make the ark.

And now, do not be distressed and
do not be angry with yourselves for selling me here,
because it was to save lives
that God sent me ahead of you.
— *Genesis 45:5*

Adventure
BIBLE

Joseph the Dreamer

Pictures by David Miles

ZONDERkidz

Joseph had a lot of brothers.

Joseph was the youngest.

And he was his father's favorite.

One day, Joseph's father gave him a robe.

It had many colors.

Joseph loved it!

When Joseph's brothers saw his robe,

they were jealous.

They asked, "Why don't we get new robes?

What makes Joseph so special?"

Then Joseph had a dream.

He told his brothers,

"Last night,

I dreamed we were picking grain.

Your bunches of grain

all bowed down to mine."

Joseph's brothers were upset.

They asked,

"Does he think he is better than us?

Does he think we should bow to him?"

They made a plan to get rid of Joseph.

One day, Joseph was out in a field.

His brothers grabbed him.

They threw him in an empty well.

Joseph was scared.
He didn't understand
why his brothers hated him,
and the well was dark.

Then someone threw down a rope.

They pulled Joseph out.

Joseph's brothers told him,

"We're selling you as a slave."

Joseph's brothers dipped his
colorful robe in goat's blood.
They showed their father.
They said,
"Your son has been killed
by a wild animal."

Joseph's father was very, very sad.

Joseph traveled with the slave traders.

They went all the way to Egypt.

In Egypt, Joseph was sold

to a rich man.

The rich man threw Joseph in jail.

Joseph hadn't even done anything wrong!

But God was with Joseph.

In jail, Joseph met a man

who used to be the king's servant.

The servant had a dream.

He said to Joseph,

"I dreamed I made a drink from grapes.

Then I gave the drink to the king.

Can you tell me what this means?"

Joseph said,

"God knows about your dream.

It means that soon

you will work for the king again."

Joseph was right.

A few days later,

the servant got out of jail.

"Don't forget about me,"

Joseph said to him.

Later, the king had a dream.

No one could tell him what it meant.

But the king's servant remembered.

"Joseph can tell you

what your dream means!" he said.

The king sent for Joseph.

He told Joseph his dream.

53

Joseph said,

"Lots of food will grow for seven years.

Then the food will stop growing.

God wants us to save food now,

so we won't be hungry later."

The king was impressed.
He put Joseph in charge
of all the food in Egypt.

Everything Joseph said came true.

For seven years lots of food grew.

Then the seven bad years began.
Even Joseph's family did not have
enough to eat.
Joseph's father sent his sons
to buy food in Egypt.

When Joseph's brothers arrived,

they bowed to Joseph.

It was just like Joseph's dream.

But they did not know

he was their brother.

Joseph knew.

Joseph sold his brothers food,

and they went home.

Later, the brothers came back
to buy more food.
They bowed to Joseph again.
This time Joseph said,
"Don't you recognize me?
I'm your brother, Joseph!"

His brothers were afraid.
Would Joseph hate them
for what they had done?

61

But Joseph said,

"I forgive you.

What you did to me was bad,

but God used it for good."

They all hugged.

The brothers rushed home.

They told their father,

"Joseph is alive!"

Soon the whole family moved to Egypt.

People of the Bible

Your father's God helps you.
He gives you blessings from the highest heaven.
— *Genesis 49:25*

Jacob

Jacob was one of Isaac's sons. He cheated his twin brother Esau out of his inheritance from their father. Jacob left home to escape his angry brother. But God promised Jacob he would watch over him wherever he went. And he was blessed with twelve sons.

Joseph

Joseph was the son of Jacob and Rachel. He was Jacob's favorite son and was treated the best. His brothers were jealous and sold him as a slave, but God used that bad thing for good. He knew that he would use Joseph to help save many people during a famine.

Life in Bible Times
Joseph's Colorful Coat

Jacob gave his favorite son, Joseph, a beautiful coat that was made with very colorful threads. Clothing like this was usually meant for special people and events. Since only Joseph got a coat like this from their father, his brothers knew he was Jacob's favorite.

God said to Moses, "I AM WHO I AM.
This is what you are to say to the Israelites:
'I AM has sent me to you.'"
—*Exodus 3:14*

Adventure BIBLE®

Moses Leads the People

Pictures by David Miles

ZONDERkidz

One day, while Moses was working

as a shepherd, he saw something odd.

It was a burning bush.

But the bush was not burning up!

Moses went to see the bush.

He heard God say, "Moses, I need your help!"

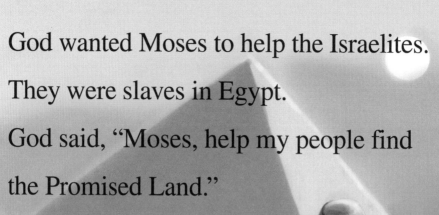

God wanted Moses to help the Israelites.

They were slaves in Egypt.

God said, "Moses, help my people find

the Promised Land."

Moses knew the Israelites.

He used to live in Egypt

and knew they suffered.

"But how can I help?" asked Moses.

God said, "I promise to help you. You

can do it!"

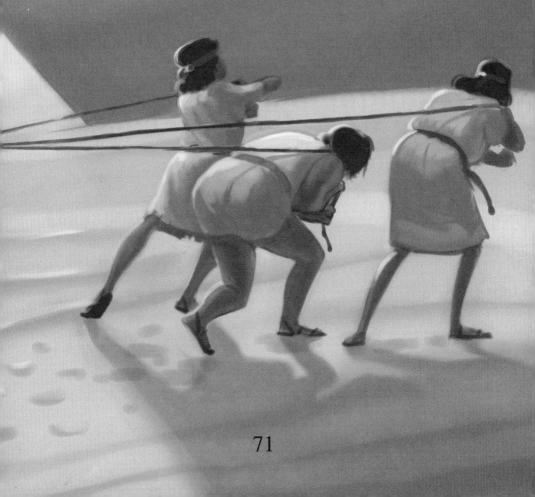

So Moses packed up and went to Egypt.

He took his family

and his brother, Aaron.

"God has blessed us both," Moses told Aaron.

"You are a good speaker.

Pharaoh will listen.

I will tell you what God wants you to say."

Moses and Aaron met with Pharaoh.

"What do you want?" Pharaoh,

the king of Egypt, asked Moses.

74

"Please let the Israelites go," said Moses.

But Pharaoh said, "No."

So God gave Moses and Aaron some tools
to use. They would convince Pharaoh.

These tools from God were called plagues.

There were ten plagues in all:

water turning to blood,

frogs,

gnats,

flies,

the death of Egyptian livestock,

77

boils,

hail,

locust,

78

darkness,

and death of each family's firstborn son.

The tenth plague was the worst.
God gave the Israelites a way to
protect their families.

God said, "Get a perfect year-old male lamb.

Take some of its blood and paint
your door frame.

Roast the lamb. Eat it with
bread made with no yeast.
Wear your traveling clothes.

If your family is too small for a whole lamb,
share with your neighbor.
Follow these directions.
No one will be hurt."

Beginning at midnight, all of the
firstborn sons of Egypt, people and
animals, were struck down.

But the Israelites who followed
God's instructions were protected.

83

That night, Pharaoh said,

"Leave Egypt now!"

The Egyptians did not want
their families hurt anymore.
They even helped the Israelites get out
of their country.

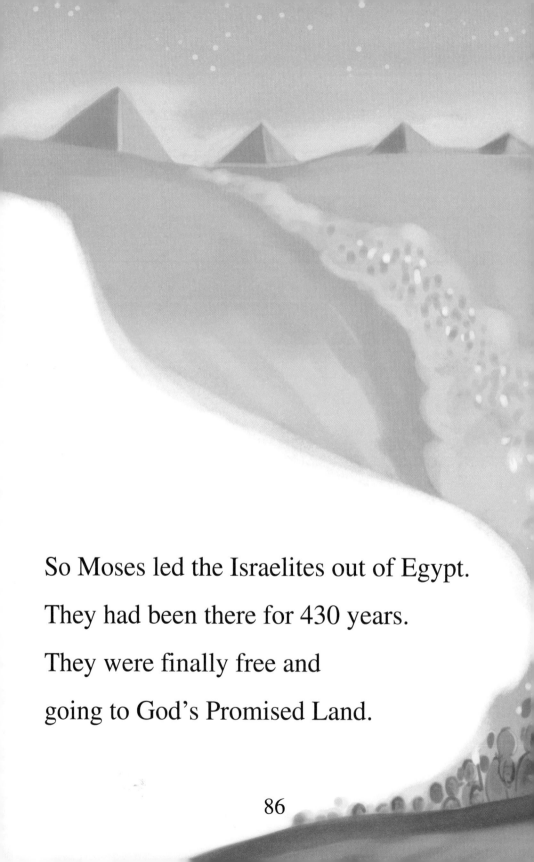

So Moses led the Israelites out of Egypt.

They had been there for 430 years.

They were finally free and

going to God's Promised Land.

God took care of Moses and the Israelites

in the desert.

He gave them a pillar of cloud to

follow by day,

and by night they followed a
pillar of fire.

After walking many days

the Israelites saw Pharaoh's army

following them.

They shouted, "What is going on?

Did you bring us to the desert to die?"

Moses replied, "Don't be afraid.
The Lord will fight for you.
Trust God."

The Israelites were near the Red Sea.

God told Moses, "Raise your staff.

Stretch out your hands and the

sea will divide."

So Moses did this.

Just as God said, the waters

were divided.

The Israelites went through the sea

on dry ground!

When they were on the other side, the

people saw the Egyptians coming.

Then the Lord said to Moses,

"Raise your hand again. The sea

will return to its place."

When Moses did, the water

went back to its place.

It covered the army and their chariots,

saving God's people.

People in Bible Times

God said to Moses, "I AM WHO I AM. This is what you are to say to the Israelites: 'I AM has sent me to you.'"
EXODUS 3:14

Moses

A Hebrew who survived Pharaoh's decree that all newborn boys must die. Moses was rescued by an Egyptian princess and raised in the palace. God chose him to be the rescuer of the Israelites from slavery in Egypt.

Aaron

He was the older brother of Moses and a noted public speaker. Aaron was the spokesman for Moses as they worked with God to free the Israelites. He was also the first high priest of Israel.

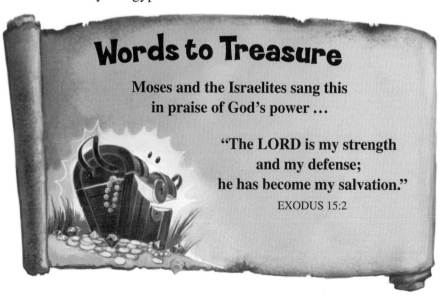

Words to Treasure

Moses and the Israelites sang this in praise of God's power ...

"The LORD is my strength and my defense; he has become my salvation."
EXODUS 15:2

All the people saw it. Then they fell down flat with their faces toward the ground. They cried out, "The Lord is the one and only God! The Lord is the one and only God!"

1 Kings 18:39

Adventure BIBLE

Elijah, God's Mighty Prophet

Pictures by David Miles

ZONDERkidz

Elijah lived in Israel,

the Promised Land

that God gave to the Jews.

Elijah was a prophet.

He was a messenger from God.

But people didn't always listen.

At that time, Ahab, the king,

did not pray to the true God.

He prayed to a god called Baal.

So did many other Jews.

Elijah made an announcement.

He said, "There will be no more rain

in Israel until I say so.

God is not happy with you."

What Elijah said came true.

The streams dried up.

Plants could not grow.

People were hungry and thirsty.

But God took care of Elijah.

God showed Elijah a stream.

God sent ravens

to bring Elijah bread and meat.

One day, Elijah saw a woman

gathering sticks.

He asked,

"Would you bring me some bread?"

The woman said, "I have no bread.

I only have a little flour and oil.

When that is gone,

my son and I will die."

Elijah told the woman,

"Go home and bake some bread.

You will not run out of flour or oil."

The woman did as Elijah said.

No matter how much oil or flour she used,

the woman did not run out.

God provided food for Elijah,

the woman, and her son.

But King Ahab was very angry.

He wanted Elijah to make it rain again.

God told Elijah

to go meet King Ahab.

When Ahab saw Elijah, he said,

"You have brought trouble!"

Elijah said,

"You have caused the trouble.

You pray to Baal.

You do not pray to the true God."

Then Elijah said,

"Call all the prophets of Baal

and all the people of Israel.

Have them meet me on Mount Carmel."

Elijah stood before the people.

He said, "How long

will you go back and forth?

If the Lord is God, follow him.

But if Baal is god, follow him."

The people said nothing.

Then Elijah said,

"Let's see who the real God is!

Let's have a contest!"

Elijah said,

"Let's put wood on two altars.

One altar is for your god, Baal.

The other altar is for my God."

"We will each call on our god.
The god who sends fire to the wood
is the true God."
The people liked this idea.

The prophets of Baal went first.

They put a bull on their altar.

They danced around

and shouted the name of Baal

from morning to noon.

In the afternoon, Elijah said,

"Maybe your god is sleeping.

Maybe he is busy.

Shout louder!"

So the prophets of Baal shouted louder.

The prophets of Baal shouted all day,

but no one answered.

Then Elijah said to the people,

"Come with me."

Elijah stood before the Lord's altar,

which had been torn down.

He used twelve stones to fix it.

He put wood and a bull on it.

He dug a trench around it.

Then Elijah told some men,

"Pour four jars of water on the wood."

They poured water on the altar.

Elijah said, "Do it two more times."

Soon the wood was very wet.

Water ran down the altar

and even filled the trench.

Everyone wondered

how the altar would burn.

Elijah stepped forward and prayed.

He said, "Lord, you are the true God,

and I am your servant.

Answer me so everyone will know

who you are!"

Fire came down from heaven!

It burned up the wood and the stones.

It burned up the bull and the soil.

It even dried the water in the trench!

When the people saw this,

they fell to their knees.

The people cried,

"The Lord is God!"

Soon after that, God sent rain.

The people could grow food

and find water again.

Elijah

Elijah was a prophet. His job was to give the people of Israel God's messages. God gave him the power to do miracles to help the people know that the Lord was the one true God.

Life in Bible Times

What exactly was a prophet in Bible times?

A prophet was person who received messages directly from God and then relayed them to God's people. This person is called by God to do this job. Sometimes the messages are God promising his everlasting love and others might be warnings to repent or try harder to follow his Word.

I'll go to the king. I'll do it even though it's against the law. And if I have to die, I'll die.
—*Esther 4:16*

I Can Read!

READING
2
WITH HELP

ZONDERkidz

Adventure BIBLE

Brave Queen Esther

Pictures by David Miles

ZONDERkidz

Once there was a woman

named Esther.

She lived with her cousin Mordecai.

Mordecai took care of Esther.

Esther and Mordecai were Jewish.

Together they loved and worshipped God.

One day the king of the land
decided to look for a queen.
"We will find you a queen,"
said the men who helped him.

The men looked all over for a new queen.

Soon they saw Esther.

"We must take her

to the king," they said.

The men brought Esther

to the palace.

The king thought Esther was

the most beautiful woman of all.

"I want you to be my queen,"

said the king.

Esther said, "Yes."

There was a great celebration.

Esther was happy.

She lived in the palace.

Esther's cousin, Mordecai,

worked in the palace.

Mordecai told Esther

to keep her faith a secret.

So Esther did not tell anyone

she and Mordecai were Jewish.

There was another man who worked
in the palace.

His name was Haman.

He helped the king.

But he hated Mordecai and wanted
to be rid of all the Jews.
Haman spoke to the king,
"The Jews are bad! We don't need them
in our kingdom."

The king trusted Haman.

He agreed to get rid of the Jews.

Mordecai heard about Haman's plan.

He went to warn Esther

and see if she would help.

Mordecai said, "Esther, you must stop the king from harming us!"

"If I go to him," Queen Esther said,

"I will get in trouble.

It is against the rules."

But Mordecai knew Esther

was the only one who could help.

"Maybe God has made you queen
so you could save the Jews,"
Mordecai said.

Esther was afraid.

She knew if she went to the

king she would be in danger.

But Esther also knew God

would want her to be brave.

She prayed for courage.

Soon Esther went to the king.

She was still scared.

But the king was happy to see Esther.

He did not punish her

for coming to him.

So Esther invited the king

and Haman to a special dinner.

"I will give you a fine feast

if it pleases you,"

Queen Esther said.

The king was happy and told her

they would be there.

Esther made a delicious meal.

Esther, the king, and Haman

sat together and ate.

Then the king asked,

"What do you want, my queen?

You can have anything."

Esther found the courage to speak.

"Please spare the Jews.

They are my people," she said.

"Mordecai told me you have been

tricked, my king."

"Tricked? By whom?" roared the king.

"Evil Haman," Esther said.

The king was angry.

"Take Haman and arrest him!"

he yelled to his guards.

"Punish him for the

bad things he has done."

Now, the king gave Mordecai
an important job in the palace.
"You are a good man, Mordecai,"
said the king. "I will trust you
more than anyone else."

All the Jews were finally safe.

God had protected them,

with the help of Mordecai and Esther.

Esther helped save the Jews
by being brave and speaking up
for God's people.
She and her cousin Mordecai
were heroes.

"Hooray!" cried the Jews.

It was a time of happiness and joy

because of brave Queen Esther.

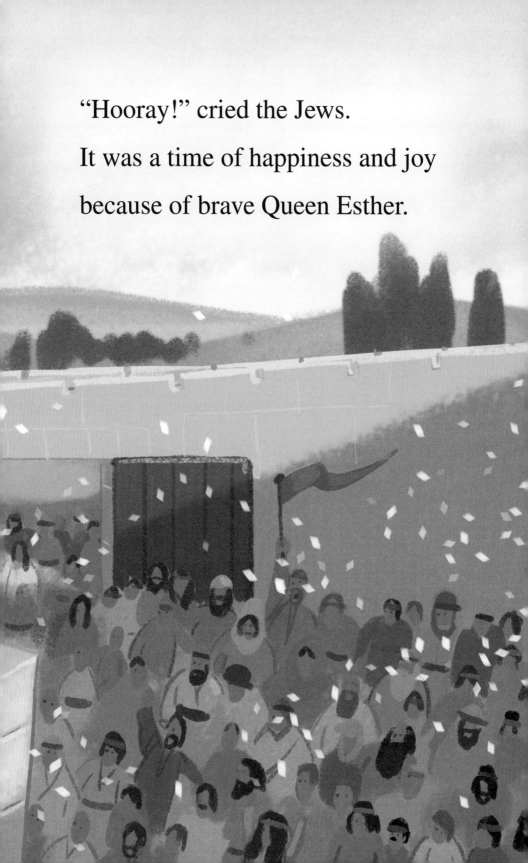

People of the Bible

Who knows but that you have come to your
royal position for such a time as this?
—*Esther 4:14*

Esther

Esther was a young Jewish woman
who lived in Persia. She became the
queen of King Xerxes. When an evil
man planned to kill all of the Jewish
people in the land, Esther prayed to
God for courage to help God's people.

Mordecai

Mordecai was a Jewish man. He had a
niece named Esther. When her parents
died, Mordecai adopted Esther to be his
daughter and loved and cared for her.
He helped Esther remember that she
could be very brave, with God's help.

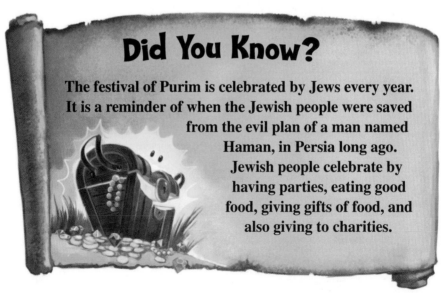

Did You Know?

The festival of Purim is celebrated by Jews every year.
It is a reminder of when the Jewish people were saved
from the evil plan of a man named
Haman, in Persia long ago.
Jewish people celebrate by
having parties, eating good
food, giving gifts of food, and
also giving to charities.

Say with your mouth, "Jesus is Lord."
Believe in your heart that God raised him
from the dead. Then you will be saved.

Romans 10:9

I Can Read!

ZONDERkidz

2

READING WITH HELP

Adventure BIBLE®

Paul Meets Jesus

Pictures by David Miles

ZONDERkidz

Saul was angry.

Not long ago,

a man named Jesus went all over the land

teaching about God.

Jesus told people

he was the Son of God.

Jesus was gone now,

but he still had many followers.

Saul did not like this.

Saul said, "The followers of Jesus
should be thrown in jail.
They are wrong.
Jesus is not the Son of God."

Saul did everything he could

to get Jesus' followers in trouble.

One day, Saul was walking

down the road.

He was on his way to a city

where followers of Jesus lived.

He wanted to arrest them.

A bright light flashed

from heaven!

Saul fell to the ground.

He was scared!

Saul heard a voice say,

"Saul, why are you trying to hurt me?"

Saul covered his head.

He asked, "Who are you?"

The voice said, "I am Jesus.

Now get up and go into the city.

You will be told what to do next."

There were some men

traveling with Saul.

They did not know what to say.

They heard the voice

but did not see anyone!

Saul got up.

When he opened his eyes,

he could not see anything!

He was blind!

His friends led him into the city.

Saul was blind for three days.

He did not eat or drink anything.

A man named Ananias lived in the city.

He loved Jesus.

One day, God spoke to Ananias
and said, "Find a man named Saul.
He is blind. Put your hands on him,
then he will be able to see."

Ananias was afraid.

He said, "God,

I have heard about Saul.

He is a bad man!

He tries to hurt Jesus' followers!"

But God said, "Go!
I chose this man.
I will use Saul to tell people
all over the world about me."

Ananias found Saul.

He placed his hands on Saul and said,

"Brother, Jesus has sent me

so that you may see again.

Be filled with the Holy Spirit."

Right away,

Saul could see again!

He got up,

and Ananias baptized him.

Saul was a new person.

He changed his name to Paul.

He believed that Jesus was God.

Paul began to teach about Jesus.

Everyone said, "Isn't this the man

who used to cause trouble

for Jesus' followers?"

But Paul didn't stop teaching.

Soon, Paul started to travel.

Sometimes he traveled with others,

and sometimes he went by himself.

Paul told everyone he met

the good news about Jesus.

In some places,

Paul was chased away.

But Paul did not give up.

In one city, there was a man

who could not walk.

He listened to every word Paul said.

Paul saw the lame man had faith.

Paul said, "Stand up!"

The man jumped up and began to walk.

The people were amazed.

Another time, Paul and his friend Silas

were thrown in jail.

God sent an earthquake.

The prison doors flew open!

Their chains fell off!

The jailer was so amazed

he asked Paul,

"What must I do to be saved?"

Paul also wrote letters.

He sent them to churches.

The letters told people

about the love of Jesus.

God changed Paul's life.

Paul became a good man.

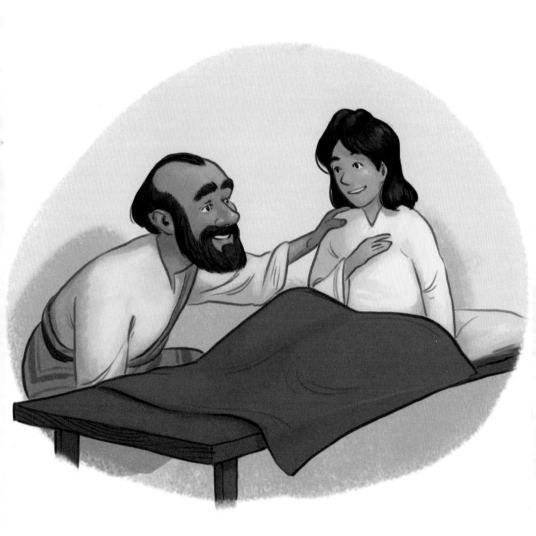

Paul preached.

He helped many people.

Paul never stopped telling people
about the love of God.

People in Bible Times

Saul/Paul

Saul was a Pharisee who hated Christians. After a miracle happened on his way to Damascus, and Jesus appeared to him, Saul became a Christian! He became a brave and powerful preacher and missionary. Paul wrote thirteen books of the Bible.

Did You Know

While Paul traveled all over the world preaching and teaching about Jesus, he did something wonderful for the believers—he prayed for them. Paul prayed for the Philippians and the Colossians and the people in Corinth. He prayed that these people, and the whole world, would grow to know and love Jesus. We can pray that same prayer for the people of the world.